To my Ninja niece and nephew,
Jessica and Max
—C.R.S.

For Jodi and Alec
—D.S.

G. P. PUTNAM'S SONS
Published by the Penguin Group
Penguin Group (USA) LLC
375 Hudson Street, New York, NY 10014

USA | Canada | UK | Ireland | Australia
New Zealand | India | South Africa | China
penguin.com
A Penguin Random House Company

Library of Congress Cataloging-in-Publication Data
Schwartz, Corey Rosen.
Ninja Red / Corey Rosen Schwartz ; illustrated by Dan Santat.
pages cm
Summary: In this twist on "Little Red Riding Hood," a certain wolf trains to be a ninja
in order to catch his prey, but he is not the only one mastering a martial art.
[1. Stories in rhyme. 2. Wolves—Fiction. 3. Martial arts—Fiction. 4. Ninja—Fiction.]
I. Santat, Dan, illustrator. II. Title.
PZ8.3.S29746Nin 2014 [E]—dc23 2013017589

Manufactured in China by South China Printing Co. Ltd.
ISBN 978-0-399-16354-8
1 3 5 7 9 10 8 6 4 2

Design by Ryan Thomann. Text set in Markin.
The art was done with Sumi brush work on rice paper and completed in Adobe Photoshop.

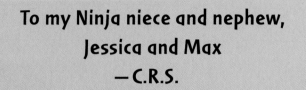

NINJA RED RIDING HOOD

Corey Rosen Schwartz

illustrated by **Dan Santat**

G. P. **PUTNAM'S SONS** • An Imprint of Penguin Group (USA)

Once upon a Ninja-filled time,

a wolf couldn't catch any prey.
He kept getting licked
by the dinner he picked
and was growing more ticked by the day.

His belly was achin' for bacon.
"I'm wasting away," he complained.
To huff and to puff
was no longer enough,

so he snuck into school to be trained.

He practiced his **katas** for hours

and mastered the **whirlwind** and **wheel.**

He jackknifed and flipped

and at **last** felt equipped

to once again catch a good meal.

The wolf licked his chops when he saw her
and hastily thought up a plan.

There are blossoms that way!
You can pick a bouquet
to give to your little old gran.

Then the wolf took a shortcut to Grandma's, where he thought that he'd find her in bed.

But Granny was gone,
so he put her robe on
and eagerly waited for Red.

Soon after, he heard someone knocking.
He called out, "**My dear, come on in.**
Oh, don't you look good
in your lovely red hood,
but a shame that you've gotten so thin."

Little Red took a look at her granny and said, "What on earth did you do? I could swear that your **eyes** have completely changed size. Hey, Gran, are you sure that it's you?"

Of course it is me, my sweet darling. The better to see you, my dear.

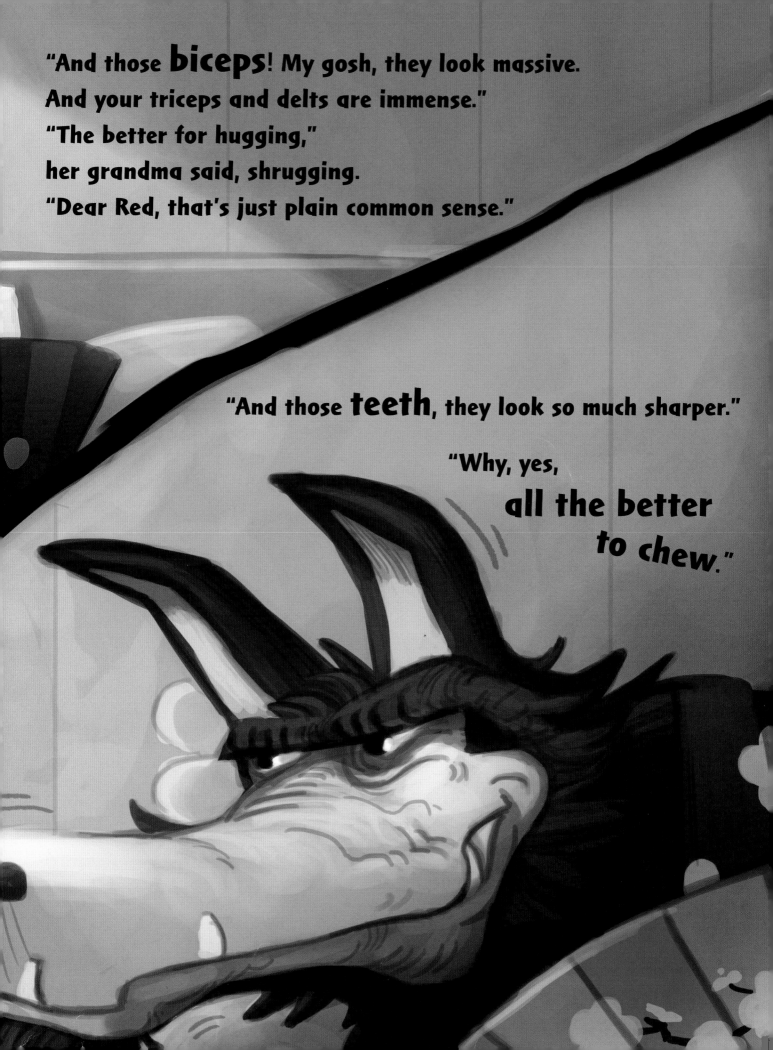

"And those **biceps**! My gosh, they look massive.
And your triceps and delts are immense."
"The better for hugging,"
her grandma said, shrugging.
"Dear Red, that's just plain common sense."

"And those **teeth**, they look so much sharper."

"Why, yes,
**all the better
to chew**."

He jumped out of bed
to gobble up Red,
    but . . .

They appeared to be evenly matched!

Just then, they both heard someone chopping.
A woodsman? Red thought. But instead—

The wolf took a swing at that instant, but Red deftly dodged the attack.

She got a good grip,
threw him over her hip,
and the wolf wound up flat on his back.

"I'll skedaddle," the wolf said in anguish
as he struggled back up on his feet.
"Just a second, you beast.
You will not be released
till you promise to give up **Red meat!**"

Though his tummy still rumbled with hunger,
the wolf faced his rival and vowed:
"Ninja Red, you have won.
My meat days are done."
"Oh, Red-chan," said Gran. "I'm so proud!"

Then Red and the wolf bowed politely,
and Gran gave him half her peach pie.
The wolf was a mess.
He'd had way too much stress.
"I guess I'll give yoga a try."

He enrolled at the Downward Dog Center,
where his tension began to decrease.
He studied with yogis,
said no to meat hoagies,
and felt, at last, truly at peace.